I0522584

Other Books

Empty Thoughts from an Empty Head
-
Observations from Another Planet
-
Stupid Jokes for Clever People & Clever Jokes for Stupid
People
-
That's the State We're In

~~~~

Books in the Logic List English Series

Logic List English – Rhyming Words etc. - Volume 1A
Logic List English – Spelling Arrangement – Volume 1B

Logic lists English - Multi-Syllable Words - Volume 2A
Logic lists English - Split Multi-Syllables - Volume 2B

More Volumes Coming
~~~~

Spaced Out
& Cut Up

A collection of Horror
& Science Fiction Short Stories

By
Tony Sandy

DragonEye Publishing

Spaced Out and Cut Up –
A collection of Horror
& Science Fiction short stories
Copyrighted © 2017 by Tony Sandy

All the characters in this book have no existence outside the imagination of the author, and have no relation whatsoever to anyone bearing the same name or names. They are not even distantly inspired by any individual known or unknown to the author, and all the incidents are pure invention.

No part of this book may be reproduced in any form or by any electronic or mechanical means including information storage and retrieval systems, without permission in writing from the author and from Publisher, with the only exception being a reviewer who may quote short excerpts in a review.

First Edition
First Printing May 5, 2017

ISBN 13: 978-1-61500-145-3 (Paperback)
ISBN 13: 978-1-61500-101-9 (ePub ebook)
ISBN 13: 978-1-61500-183-5 (PDF)

Library of Congress Control Number: 2017940168

Published by Canned Horror, an Imprint of DragonEye Publishing

Contact info
DragonEyePublishers.com
Orders@DragonEyePublishers.com

DragonEye Publishing
753 Linden Place, Unit A
Elmira, NY 14901 USA

Table of Contents

INTRODUCTION

Welcome to a world, populated by creatures not ruled by man, that consider him food for thought (or a local delicacy, in the crossover horror/ science fiction story that starts the next section). From this point on it is all downhill, even if sometimes in an amusing way (but not if you're the one being eaten of course).

These stories end up on a more happy note, in the realm of the future, where robots rule and new worlds have been conquered by man, so it's not all bad, unless you've seen Alien, Predator, The Thing, Invasion of The Body Snatchers....

These are mostly quick reads for commuters on their way to or from the biggest horror of all – work or if adventurous, a journey to elswhere / else when in the universe. Wherever they take you, they cannot be *ignored* even if you're being *gnawed* at the time, by some zombie on his way to work too (or blood sucker, if it's management).

Without further ado...

THE ZOMBIE DIARIES OR 'WE'RE SORRY FOR YOUR LOSS'

When I died, I never realized how much it would change my life. I don't miss the sex. I look down and think easy come, easy go. Food though, that's different. I can't taste anything, anymore but I have this indescribable yearning for warm, living flesh. Once upon a time it was fine wines, delicate flavours. What did these things taste like I will never know. I can't remember anything much about my previous existence, especially with regards to the basic senses. Everything about my life is so vague, so unreal nowadays. It's good losing all those memories. I no longer feel the pain of the past. All the emotional hurt I caused, lost in a fog of indifference. I don't feel in the other way either. I was hit by a speeding car, driven by a crazed driver, eager to get away from me. I just picked myself up, dusted myself down and walked off like nothing had happened. This road rage incident would normally have had me hospitalised. Why the panic I wondered? He could have run faster than me any day. In fact he could have walked faster as well: We can only catch others when we hunt in packs or catch them unawares (asleep, eating, in the toilet, panicking to get out of a door or a window and fumbling at the latch or handle).

Life makes no 'scents' to me anymore. I hear werewolves are the opposite. Smell is heightened but not in my case. I may stink because I'm composed of decomposing flesh but I can't tell (Even your best friends won't tell you). Rotten sense of taste, smell, touch - can't see or hear well either. I'm rotten all round.

The only thing I can sense is warmth. I suppose that's because I'm 'dead' cold...heartless even or at least dead beat. Shuffling along city streets or country roads, all I see are my dead brothers and sisters, shuffling along just as pointlessly. Is there no hope left for Man? Are we the remnants of a despairing God? Can this be humanities fate - more of us, less of them? We hate the living for what they have because we don't have it anymore. They live and breathe in their rarity, while we suffocate in our monstrous numbers. We starve in our limitations and drown in our abundant nothingness. Empty of promise, we have no future. Our children won't follow us except into oblivion. We rot in our our empty shells of yesterday as though today meant something (It doesn't). What is there to say? Nothing. What is there to do? Likewise nothing. So instead of living meaningful lives, we die in meaningless ones instead. The ground could not hold us because we bored it to death. Slow moving? Slow thinking too. We are in no rush to get anywhere, do anything. We are the ultimate in laid back. Who set the alarm that got us up, I wonder? Where are we going? nowhere. What are we doing? Nothing in particular. We are the inheritors of a dead kingdom - the land of the hippies. Oh God, am I still here, still alive in this dead body? Is there no release from this wasted, wasted life....

I'm so exhausted. I wish I could sleep but that's a luxury reserved for the living. Even vampires sleep but then they're not properly alive either are they? Oh the delicate actions I used to perform, like lifting up a fork. If I tried that now, I'd knock the table flying. I suppose that I don't sleep because I don't run off off my excess energy (As I don't have any, how can I?). We're stuck in limbo as a race - always present but never really here, never really aware. I grunt and groan at every movement. I growl at the dogs that try to pull me down or run off with various body parts. Stairs? I hate stairs! Even Daleks never had the problem I have with them. You corner a human, go all the way up to the landing and they've jumped out the window by the time you've reached them. Still it's not always bad news. Sometimes we stumble all the way back down again, to find them lying outside, unconscious or staggering away with a broken leg: Oh goody, equal footing! It's a bit like fishing but we don't have any bait, although I do remember a particularly smart guy for a zombie, who went from supermarket to supermarket, for his weekly shop. Well weekly might be too short a time span to describe his hunting patterns. We are like reptiles. We don't need to eat daily - just every now and again. That grumbling in my tummy for instance is the late Reverend Jenkins. It's funny to think I dined on him last night, rather than with him as I used to do on the odd occasion.

Inner life? I don't have an inner life. My attention span has gone, so books are out of the question - besides I can't turn individual pages (as I say, delicate movement has gone). I remember some poor guy trying to imitate someone reading. The book fell to bits in his hands. It was almost as funny as this zombie trying to have sex with another zombie (a half remembered activity from another time - like a child trying to act like an adult and failing miserably or a monkey mimicking a human). The strangest part was the zombie woman, who first of all ignored his advances, then tried to push him off as she got on with eating a passing stranger. Then a light of recognition seemed to flicker inside her as she realized what he was trying to do. She turned towards him, took his face in her hands and bit him. He soon got the message as much as if they were a live couple - not tonight darling, I'm dining out with friends.

I have to watch myself. I have this old habit of picking at my skin, when nervous. I stripped the flesh off my left arm one night (lose bit and I pulled until it reached my elbow). Won't do that again. Forgot it doesn't grow back anymore.

I feel drunk all the time. It's like I stagger all over the place, hardly able to control my movements. The worst thing is the permanent hangover aspect of it all (the stomach permanently out of sorts and the headache). I want to poke my fingers into my eyes, just to get at the source of the pain but I know it would blind me and there's nothing worse than being a blind, hungry zombie.

Talking of fine dining and alcohol, I sometimes wish I were a vampire. They at least can walk into a restaurant without anyone batting an eye - me, I'd have to shuffle round the back and dig through the bins, for something to eat as tramps wouldn't get through the front door.

'No tie sir and no skin on your left arm. Sorry we cannot let you in like that, besides which the smell of decaying flesh would put the other diners off.' I can hear it all now. Vampires however could drink delicate flavoured red wine and get away with it. Eating though might be a problem. Steak, rare, with blood oozing out. How could they resist the urge to pick it up and suck it dry? Us monsters always show ourselves up in refined company. I of course shouldn't be in the ranks of the decaying.   With my breeding really I should be underground, only coming out at night to dine on the best necks in town. Alas it was not meant to be.

Werewolves. I always keep an eye on the moon in case it's full. I remember one band of zombies I came upon, who'd obviously thought they'd cornered a nice, juicy meal out in the open, when it turned out that it had cornered and opened them up instead (No blood but plenty of guts and limbs spread everywhere). I remember one poor fellow - his decapitated head, still blinking in disbelief at what had just happened.

It's a disgusting, pain filled life but I have no choice, except to lead it. I could kill myself and I've seen the results of, some of the recently turned - heads torn off, when they tried to hang themselves. Others still 'alive' but smashed up, when they stood in front of a train or lorry (glancing blow survivors). Standing head on was very effective as you can imagine - spectacular even. Humpty-Dumpty had a great Fall but getting hit by a truck took the Spring out of his step, leaving him with egg all over his face. The good thing though is that it did bring him out of his shell.

When I say we have no inner life as you can see that isn't strictly true. I've seen zombies who were as daft as my dogs, before I ate them. Trying to negotiate a narrow gap, instead of turning sideways as any normal monster would do, they'd keep trying to go through, head on. Bash, bash, bash without learning a thing. I wanted to just grab their shoulders and turn them forty five degrees but I'd already found that didn't work as they'd then go in the direction they were now orientated in. They were like these toys that used to bounce off the skirting board, turn and head in a new direction ad infinitum or like mindless zombies, which of course is what they were. I suppose the fact I started off more educated and well brought up, put me at a distinct advantage over my fellow dead-heads (I'd got further to fall, more to lose).

Do we live forever? No. We cannot regenerate decaying matter, so eventually fall by the wayside - our losses more than made up for by the living, when death takes them by the hand. What I fate I often think. To die, thinking you're heading for paradise and instead to wake up back here again, still alive but in a more meagre way. We who are about to die, salute you! (or we will do when we rise again).

I can still remember my first kill. That mouthful of warm flesh was so good. I was on the outskirts of the pack - a know nothing newbie, given the chance to join in. As I said, we cannot taste but we can sense warmth. I bit into that still screaming, still living human being. We tore her to pieces, until blood loss knocked her unconscious. A part of me wanted to scream 'No!'

Another part of me wanted to vomit - revolted and ashamed at what I'd done but the hunger was too strong. It's an addiction all living things have and we are no different. We eat to survive.

One of the crowd looked at me afterwards as much as to say you did alright kid, you're now fully bloodied. I grunted in acknowledgement and turned away satisfied. In an earlier incarnation this would have come across as a smile, a raised glass or even a pat on the back. We sat down afterwards. like everyone does after a good meal. Being zombies though, we could not afford to settle for long because like the Tin Man in The Wizard of Oz, you froze as rigor mortis set in. Joints cracked as we rose and some whose time had come, never rose again (We didn't even give them a backwards glance as they sat and rotted in the clearing, their eyes being the only sign of life: For those of us who came back to life, there was the rising. For those returning to dust, there is only the settling or the crumbling).

It might be more accurate to say that inner life is all I have rather than that I have none. No intelligible sounds come out of my mouth and my interaction with the outside world is minimal. I grunt and groan at the others but that is as far as it goes. I'm introverted because I don't have the energy (or body parts) to extrovert; no deep philosophical discussions or even idle chit-chat.

'Morning Mrs Wicks, how's your lumbago?'

'Hi Fred, where's Marge this morning?'

I would kill, even to say something as trite as this, where once I'd turn my nose up at such a waste of time and effort (Nowadays I see the world through a glass, darkly).

I have no future and a quickly disappearing past. The present is dull as ditch water and smells as stagnant. I am nothing in a sea of nothingness. It's a man's life in the army - well it's a nothing life as a zombie. The same boring nothingness, day after day, interrupted only by the occasional meal. We're like reptiles, eating now and again but resting the rest of the time. Have I said that before? Then the degeneration is complete and my mind is now going, rotting faster than my body. The circular life of the bored and boring is becoming my own. I will repeat every day as if it were every other day and my last bastion of hope, my memory, my awareness, will fade into the twilight world I inhabit; neither alive nor dead, asleep nor awake; conscious nor unconscious. A thing barely alive but annoyingly so to those who are still in charge of their faculties, still really alive: Those that can smell Spring's flowers, taste the air, eat snow flakes, touch and be touched by love; drink in every day as if it were your last and in our case wish it were...

CULTURE SHOCK

I was lost, asleep, caught in a nightmare, until Professor Andrews rescued me. His treatment was new, radical and no-one else had thought of it, let alone tried it. I was the first successful guinea pig - all the others had 'died' or remained unchanged but I was saved. The current was too strong, too weak or the condition of the others was too far gone. After the series of shocks, I started to remember who I was, who I'd been before and then I was slowly able to communicate this to others. "My name is Charles Ward," I said, stumblingly.

"I used to live in Acacia Avenue, Fulham. I was married with two children, until the illness took me. My family - God no! Were my first victims (I would have cried, had it been physically possible but my condition stopped me).

"It's alright old man. Steady on. It's perfectly understandable. The horrors of your previous life," said the professor.

He was the only one who treated me with kindness. The others in the establishment called me a monster and didn't trust me.

"Once one of them, always one of them," they intoned behind my back.

"You just can't trust them - I wouldn't turn my back on him for a second."

I was still a monster, a misfit to them and would revert to type, given half a chance. Maybe they were right - how could I tell? I could be fine one minute and slide back into bad habits in an instant - who knows? Even the professor can't be sure, which is why I'm monitored so thoroughly. The cameras pan me. Eyes follow my every move. If it wasn't for the recovered memories of who I was, I might become paranoid.

My beautiful daughters! My wife! How could I do this horrible thing to them? I was a monster alright. A creature not to be trusted. I was an addict of human flesh and the professor had saved me.

They give me insulin and feed me nutrients, intravenously because they say I cannot digest food normally yet. Apparently all the dead flesh is returning to life and I am becoming 'human' again. They say the return to conscious awareness is the first stage and that they might be winning this war, if they can turn me back to normality. The professor believes that consciousness is what keeps the animal urges under control and stops me - us in fact, from being condemned to a life of mindless cannibalism, eternally. I hope he is right. He further believes (and the evidence seems to suggest it, strongly) that once you've captured the mind and got it in thrall, the body will follow. He says, like criminals and addicts, it's a question of reprogramming the being.

I really hope he is right.

The guards wanted their revenge on me - not for my crimes against my own flesh and blood but for those they had lost to 'my kind.' It gave them a sense of closure and of power, to beat the hell out of me. It made little to me as I felt nothing and was broken already, in mind and spirit, and as the professor said the body just followed down the mineshaft of terror.

I am not alone here. The others are chained and locked in cells because they have been known to gnaw off their own hands and pull off their own feet, to try to escape - such is the effect of their deep hunger. They look at me with pleading eyes - like animals that cannot communicate in any other way. I turn my back on them, glad to no longer be one of their number, sad that they are still trapped in this lifestyle and ashamed that I cannot help these lab rats.

Talking of lab rats, the urge is returning in me. It started with surreptitiously swallowed insects, then rodents, birds if I can catch them and once a hedgehog. Oh yes, as they learned to trust me, they let me out into the grounds - at first supervised, then quite freely. By this time Andrews had moved on. I was no longer his favourite 'pet,' just an old project that he let others monitor. I was still fenced in. I still had cameras aimed at me but by this time I was considered mostly harmless. The smell of rotting flash that was me, had subsided with time and the effects of various treatments. On top of that people had become acclimatised to my odour. I was the grenade that hadn't gone off.

Now, like a prisoner of war, I searched for a weak point - the spot where the searchlights or cameras missed and I dug.

I had known I was starting to revert when the Parkinson's like symptoms started to reappear and I found it hard to kick start my body into normal, human motion. I hid the shuffling gait as best as I could, the creeping catatonia but I knew the condition was returning and that there was no point fighting it.

I saw my people wandering in large, distant herds. I heard the sound of gunfire and explosions as the humans culled them. I longed to join them. I wanted to forget the normality I'd been a part of in the past and rejoined here: The bright light effect of coming out of a cinema into daylight, the noise, the smells, the sensitivity of touch and above all 'taste.' I wanted to forget all of these plus the memories of what I'd done to others, who trusted me to be at least 'human.' The wounds of these half remembered crimes against what I was, was just too much to bear. I wanted to slip back into the opulent dark of unknowing. To be without that sharpness of conscience and consciousness, was all I longed for. I wanted to forget, big time and tonight my opportunity came. I scrambled under the wire and got away, joining my brothers and sisters of the flesh. At first they sniffed me, like some new animal but then realised I was still the same underneath. Soon the zombie army marched on, with me in its midst. Sorry professor but I must remain true to my calling as you do yours. You didn't sin against what you were but for me there is no going back and no desire to. Even now the language centre is going and with it my mind.

"Ugh, snarl, grunt."

MOCK ZOMBIE

They told me it would happen but I didn't believe them (more fool me). I was young, optimistic, naive. Then it started ...

First came a subtle change in my awareness of scent. I noticed that I smelled differently - almost overnight. I no longer had that odour I associated with the previous me. I was wholesome - how could this strange smell of decay be me? Nobody commented but I could tell they'd noticed as once I'd have noticed it in others too. They were alien to me and now I was alien to them but not in a bold, obvious way.

Then came taste as an equally primitive manifestation. Food didn't satisfy me as it had. It became tasteless pap. I yearned for something more to satisfy me but nothing did.

I noticed my sight getting more blurry and I couldn't stand bright light. I looked in the mirror. Was this vacant expression really mine? Other people and the world in general seemed less real to me.   People snubbed me, even if they knew me. Others laughed at me or ignored the changed person I'd become. Some looked at me with disgust or horror, fearing one day this might be their fate.

My body stumbled as did my mouth too. My faculties were slipping as was the control of my body. Accidents happened daily because I longer connected with the world as I had formerly. Slow, staggered movements wrecked my body's fluidity of movement. My mind, once sharp, was now a blunt instrument (recall was negligible or totally absent). My talk was vague, faltering as my brain crumbled into oblivion within its bony cage.

It was starting to become obvious to others that I was no longer my old self but my wife refused to accept it.

"Ruby lets go! He's becoming a danger to himself and everyone else around him - and that means you too!"

"I won't give him up! My Jim, my Jim..."

"Ruby, he's not your Jim anymore!"

And with that my brother-in-law arranged my collection, to save his sister from the violent rages that were part of my condition.

They keep me locked in here now. The nurses control our behaviour through various drugs and physical restraint where necessary. Because I don't talk doesn't mean I don't think. I'm locked in this rotting shell and nobody can hear me screaming in rage and helplessness.

I won't forget you, you bastards! You think I'm not aware of the brutal, dehumanizing treatment I receive at your hands?   You think I'm a mindless, inhuman monster? Well don't turn your back on me in contempt or you'll find out how alive I am!

One day I'll...we'll break out of here - then watch out! You can't treat us like this forever and get away with it. One day the old and decrepit like me will rise up and revolt, then we'll see how much you care home carers, really care!

ROMERO'S CHILDREN

When it first started, the authorities didn't know what to do with these shambling, mindless
automatons, so they gathered them together and put them in what they euphemistically called
'homes.' As time went by they began to outnumber and overrun the general population. The world
filled with their kind and humankind found itself fighting a losing battle. They filled the streets,
then whole towns and cities - even the countryside eventually wasn't safe. All they did, day and night, was wander aimlessly around as grim parodies of their former selves. They knew that they used to be something, do something and yearned to remember what but could now only reflect a shallow version of that life, in a pitiful imitation. Like children, trying to act like adults, they wandered through streets and towns in a horrific dumb show of what it meant to be human.

Within a few years they swamped humanity, like some vast tidal wave of imbecility. The military of course thought bombing them to hell would reduce their numbers and when that didn't work, they tried the nuclear option and found that backfired: They fried hundreds of thousands, of them but their own populations of normal people, got sick and died from radiation poisoning, worldwide; joining the ranks of living dead and replacing their numbers in droves. The scientists tried this, then that and eventually gave up, after making no headway. The politicians of course talked the hind legs off a donkey and made no difference either (surprise, surprise).

Eventually it became like a scene from the film of HG Wells's 'Time Machine,' only with The Eloi retreating to the caves and barricading themselves in for protection and the monsters surrounding them night and day.

We helped them as best as we could. They were in our domain now and shocked into silence, like the humans in 'Planet of The Apes' - their pride shattered. They are our cattle and we tend them as best as we can. We put them out to pasture during the day, to eat whatever humans eat and take them back in at night, so we can feed off them. They are our breeding stock. How ironic to think that they hunted us to near extinction and now here we are - their saviours, rescuing them from being wiped out by the new dominant force on the Earth. So, you didn't need us and now you do! Life turns full circle. Like Masai warriors, we just take the blood - for the blood is the life and we'll survive in this symbiotic relationship, forever more. I'd stake my life on it.

I WAS A TEENAGE ZOMBIE

When I first died, my parents weren't too put out. I still smelled as bad - well maybe a bit worse because of the rotting flesh. My room was still a shambles. I still wandered around like the undead (no change there then). Still grunted and moaned instead of 'talked like any normal human being' as my mum would say.

Ralph next door was still my friend, although he'd turned after being bitten by a werewolf. Jeff, the other side of me, was a different kettle of fish. Since he'd been necked by a vampire, he was just 'too good' to speak to me. He'd literally gone up in the world and it had gone to his head I suppose. He frequented night clubs and dropped out of school. He said he was still in education but that I wouldn't understand. He was right, the stuck up bastard! One bite on the neck and he was anybody's but mine. Mr Drushka, his mentor, said I'd get over it as 'Jeffrey' moved in different circles now.

"Like vultures over a corpse?" I said.

"No, we feed off the living - hence he couldn't associate with you anymore as you are so obviously dead." With that he sniffed the air in disgust.

"Snobs the lot of you!" I fumed but wished I hadn't as it gave me a headache.

"Different paths my boy, just different paths. Many apply but few are chosen. Now shuffle off you smelly urchin, you're frightening off dinner."

I saw my mum leaning over the fence, talking to his mum one day.

"He always was a night owl - now he's worse. Won't get out of bed before sundown. Won't get in his coffin before daybreak. I'm dead worried Joan and that crowd he hangs about with now, they're right up their own backsides - not like your Dave's friends. At least he gets out in the daylight and his friends are near enough normal as teenagers, even if they smell a bit. That boy is a worry to me. I keep on at him about his education and he says don't get your knickers in a twist ma, I'm getting all the learning I need at night school, besides I've got all the time in the world. So I say, you're not getting any younger and he says I'm not getting any older either and smirks. Oh I could have knocked that smile off his face!"

"I know Carol. Mrs Wilson at 28 had the same problem with her girl, Samantha and tried to slap some sense into her but her hand went right through her face."

"Ghost?"

"Yes but at least that's nearly normal isn't it? Won't leave home. Says she can't or she'll become a wandering soul, like The Flying Dutchman - whoever he was. She says she's sure her mum wouldn't want that."

"Jean's Clive turned from a Goth into a werewolf - you'd never know the difference!

They both laughed.

"Margery at number 40 had her daughter turn into a vampire too. At least it stopped Lucy gawping in the mirror every five minutes, worrying about her appearance. That girl and her make up! Her mum said she had a right temper tantrum when she first turned and realized she couldn't see herself anymore! She was so livid about not being able to see her own reflection, she stormed out of the house and tried to bite the first person she came to but because they had garlic in their pocket, she bit someone else instead!"

They roared with laughter at the thought.

It's hard being a teenager at the best of times but when you're in my state, it's ten times worse. For instance I had to split from my girlfriend because her mum didn't like the fact I found her good enough to eat (and tried to on several occasions).

Well that's my life since I died anyway.

I WALK ALONE

These lonely streets - how many years have I walked them, seeking solace? I remember when they were mud, then cobble stones, now tarmac. I have lived hundreds of years and rarely met my own kind. We are solitary creatures that need none but our own company, most of the time.

I flit from town to town, needing only to return to my 'nest' by dawn. We have survived as we are because of what we are. Our style of life and the fact that we are an elite in the pecking order, means we don't associate and cannot associate with others, for survival sake.

As night owls we hide in the dark as our prey frequent the daylight hours and each others company as befits cattle. The solitary hunter knows safety lies in the dark shadows. We lie in wait, then pounce on our prey but in a more subtle way than the lion or other animal predator does. We don't want our victim frightened, so that they bolt. We need them quiescent, obliging, calm for our coup de grace (The gentle art of lovemaking only a vampire can complete). We don't want them dead, just a little bit drained, so that they can recover for the next time. We don't seek to populate more of our number than need be or who will we feed off, if the world is full of our own kind and nothing else? We try to maintain a ratio between them and us, so that they don't feel threatened enough by our existence, to try to wipe us out. Nor do we let our numbers drop to the point where we are no threat to their existence, should they revolt against us: Like mosquitoes we don't push our luck and become such noticeable nuisances that Mankind acts to reduce our strength.

We are wise - not beyond our years but because of them. We have all the time in the world and use it to our advantage. We usually entice to get our way but force, in the form of hypnotic stare or straightforward deception, is not unknown. Violence is desperation and this is the opposite of our stance. Like fishermen or spiders in their webs, we wait patiently for our prey to blunder into our trap. Once that happens, we reel them in (Spiders mummify their victims - not us as for we are already and voluntarily entombed for our own protection and survival).

You'll excuse me now as I must say hello to somebody I occasionally meet. Like me she's a street walker but of a different kind. I enjoy her mind and ready wit - and no, when we go for a bite, it is so that she can eat something solid, not that I can imbibe something liquid: I take the odd glass of wine, in memory of long forgotten history or even coffee to appear normal but I can't see why anyone in their right mind would want to drink it otherwise.

'O tempora! O mores!' as my great uncle Cicero would say.

THE ACCIDENT

She was dead. I'd seen it happen with my own two eyes but nobody else would believe it.

'You must be mistaken.'

'Not her!'

But I was there, they weren't. I'd seen the car appear out of nowhere and bowl her over - mangling her bloody corpse as it dragged her along the road and carried on as if nothing had happened.

She was dead. Of course it could have been someone else that was this bloody, unrecognisable mess now but it was definitely her that had stepped off the curb and tried to run across the open road - playing chicken with her life. It was her for certain and she was definitely dead - the second car that hit her, unknowingly, made sure of that. Thud, bump and that was that. She might have moved a little before that but not this time - not this second hit that was anything but glancing.

She was dead alright. A mangled excuse for a living being.

What could you say to her relatives, her friends? She was hot headed and paid for it? Would they thank you for such a truthful obituary?

I looked at the road, expecting someone to come - someone else to see what had happened but this was the countryside not the town. This was where death was commonplace, even if not acknowledged. Animals died everyday - killed by human hand. The cities of course were filled with every wickedness possible - you expected death and cruelty there but here it was just acknowledged as part of life, not judged. This was the countryside's practical viewpoint of that was just how things were versus the idle entertainment of towns where things like that, should or shouldn't be in people's opinion.

She was dead alright and I'd seen it. Should I just accept it and get on with my own life? What choice did I have? Only the living suffer - the dead are beyond it. She was dead and gone - and that was that. She'd been a lovely young thing when alive but like all overconfident, joyful creatures, she took unnecessary risks and didn't see any danger in the world. Death though, waited for her patiently, knowing that all he had to do was bide his time and just be prepared to catch her, when she fell from grace: We all make mistakes after all...

She was definitely dead. Those cold, black sightless eyes stared perpetually at the stars and all daylight was now darkness to her. Blood ran through her slightly opened mouth. Rivers of red tears, trickled from the corner of her left eye. Her head crushed by the wheels of one or both cars. Her limbs, contorted in a dance of death, that spun her through the air, scraping her legs across the rough, gravelly surface of the granite track. The wind blew dust across her distorted form - ashes to ashes, dust to dust...

Who couldn't mourn the loss of such a young life, cut short so tragically? I felt nothing but sorrow for her as she felt, thankfully, nothing herself. That gentle face would soon rot into a lifeless skull, unrecognisable to anyone who knew her. The bones would further descend into dust, to be blown into the faces of other road traffic victims. The young and foolish never learn - the wise aged, never forget.

She was dead, oh yes she was dead...my doe, eyed doe. My wild and free one, my fellow rabbit...

VAMPIRES

Two vampires met again after several years.
"Orloff!"
"Yuri!"
"I haven't seen you in years - you haven't aged a bit!"
"How are you?"
"Oh, mustn't crumble."
"Nice Tux!"
"Thanks!"
"Fancy stopping here for a quick bite?"
"Okay"
"Like a steak?"
"You must be kidding!"
"More garlic?"
"Of course not!"
"Oh look over there, it's Van Helsing - shall we say hello?"
"I don't think so. I see your sense of humour is as irrepressible as ever"
"Talking of the Professor. Did you hear that story about him?"
"No."
"Well, just before he died, Peter Sellers was bitten on the neck by one of us. Van Helsing, hearing of this, immediately rushed to his graveside, Dug open the casket and popped up the lid. Suddenly a voice piped up

inside-
    'Is that you Spike?'
    'Well, sort of'
Thud!"
"That's the best joke I've heard in centuries!"
"They say Sellers was a bit mean."
"Really?'
"Yes, trying to get money from him was like trying to get blood from a stone."
"Keith Richard or Mick Jagger?"
"No idea." There was a pause.
"Here's another. What does a vampire's victim say when they first meet?"
"I don't know"
"I've been dying to meet you for years!"
"Don't give up the day job!"
They both laughed and with that said their goodbyes.
"Must fly!'
"Me too"
And disappeared into the night.

CANNIBAL MARKET

"Roll up, roll up! Get your five a day here! Support your local butchers!"

"Yes love, what can I get you?"

"We're going on a picnic - got any pickled legs or Gurkhas?"

"No but I've got some ham burglars."

"No thanks. How about picnic eyeballs?"

"No, I'm afraid I only have eyes for stew"

"Pity" She paused and looked down, ready to give up.

"I could do you some Sam wedges, finger food, cheese and bunion crisps..."

"No."

"How about a nice Kate and Sidney pie?"

"No thanks. Got any missionaries or knights?'

"You mean meals on wheels or canned meat? Sorry fresh out. If it's foreign food you're after, we've got a special - buy Juan, get Wong free."

She laughed.

"You're a bit of an entrepreneur, aren't you?"

"That's a big word but yes I do have a finger in every pie, so to speak."

"I'd heard you butchered your posh friend and chopped him up for dog food."

"Oh you mean my pedigree chum. Rumours, just rumours."

"Well I think I'll leave it today."

With that she waltzed off, happy at the banter, if nothing else.

BUTCHERS

They had travelled so far across the universe that a great hunger and thirst for something real to eat and drink had enveloped them, like nothing on Earth. Countless eons, eating nothing but pills and synthetic slop, had made them as a race, long for anything to break the monotony. Then they sighted the planet and saw that it had abundant plant and animal life on it.

They landed and and feasted on all the delights of the senses that these millennia of space travel had denied them. They breathed in fresh air and tasted the many subtle particles, buoyed up by this collection of gases. They felt the textures of rock, soil and sand beneath their feet. Their hands ran through the cool water and grass. They looked at all the colours and interplays of light - the reds, the browns, the greens... They listened to the myriad of sounds around them; then the killing began.

They cleared the land for their habitation - chopping down trees, burning down bushes and grass. Destroying any creature, too slow to move out of the way in time or too inquisitive, to keep out of the way.

They could breathe the atmosphere with little trouble. As they discovered, most water could be safely drunk or filtered from the sea. Swampy water carried all kinds of poisonous micro-organisms or toxins.

There was a frenzy for fresh meat, fruit and vegetables from the civilian population, once released upon the planet. Many died or were made seriously ill initially because not all plants were safe to eat and some of the animals were poisonous or fought back too. The government, which consisted of the ruling council from the armada, restricted the worst excesses of this feeding frenzy, while the scientists checked out what was safe to eat and what was not.

Many hundreds of years passed and vast tracts of land on the various continents, were cleared. Deserts were made to artificially bloom. Jungle was turned into grassland and vast herds of animals were domesticated. Within a few hundred years the planet was conquered...

"Morning neighbour - where are you off to?"
"The Butchers. Fancied a a side of beef and maybe a bit of loin. Yourself?"
"You know me, I'm a vegetarian. Can't stand anything sentient suffering."
"How do you know they suffer - they're only bits of meat, fit for nothing but eating."
"Well that's your opinion - mine is different."

With that the pair parted company - Sammo, to the

butchery department of his local store and Denko to maintaining his garden, saying to himself "You don't eat kith and kin."

In he walked, proudly waiting for his turn to order.

"I'll have some of that. One of those and can I have a hand?"

"Just one?" asked the butcher behind the counter. "They're on special this week - two for the price of one."

"One will do, thank you"

"White, black, brown or yellow?"

"White please. I find the others tend to be a bit salty for my taste."

"Hot countries bring it to the surface. This one okay?"

"Fine."

"Do you want me to pull the nails out?"

"Yes please. The wife doesn't like doing it for some reason."

"Most people are the same"

And with that he ripped them out, with the alien equivalent of pliers.

"You should hear them squeal when they do that at the piggery. Personally I think it's cruel but the farmer says it's necessary as it stops them fighting and gouging each others eyes out - and you know what delicacies eyeballs are, don't you?"

"Yes."

"Anything else?"

"No thanks."

"That's fifteen Sturkels."

Sammo paid the credits in the usual manner and walked happily home. The chopped up thighs would do for the weekend barbecue but the pickled fingers and palm would do for his work lunch. The rest would go in the freezer.

"Fancy Denko missing out on such treats?" He thought to himself.

ALMOST HUMAN

'Getting to know you, getting to know all about you!'

How ironic this song now sounds.

When we first came to this planet, we'd been travelling for millennia of your time. Our planet had been destroyed, when our sun went super nova. We piled into our spacecraft and searched the universe for a new home, where we would be welcome (again how ironic).

Our first contacts with your world, led to an exchange of technology and the development of secret underground bases, where some of our people could live and work in peace, cementing the relationships with our new hosts. Although we were only a few hundred thousand, we needed more room than even these hidden places could provide. Our forward bases provided us with data for colonisation and now, fifty years later, we are here in force on this planet.

It started with internment camps all over the Earth. It was thought best to slowly acclimatise the local inhabitants - firstly to our existence, then to us physically being here.

Reactions? The heaven and hell of integration. The vast majority were apprehensive - wondering and checking us out all the time (hoping for the best but expecting the worst - disease, war, famine).

Some hated beyond belief - others loved but just a little too much and in a creepy, perverted kind of way. I don't know which is worse - overly curious or overtly hostile.

It's easier to kill or destroy that which is new, strange, than struggle to understand it. Some of us have embraced these differences between us and seen it as a challenge worth exploring and exploiting; others want to leave now, this instant and wish we'd never landed.

We are an old race. We expected difficulties. we see it in our own people, let alone our relationship to others.

Your prejudices cast their shadow over many areas of your lives: City and country folk; rich and poor; male and female; young and old; straight and homosexual, left and right wing politics, left and right handed; ginger haired and blond; black and white - your smell, your looks, your clothes, your beliefs and now you've got us - a whole new ball game, a whole new race of beings to love or hate, mend or break, blend in with or reject and eject from your lives (new fears to overcome or to overcome you).

The world governments fought hard to keep our existence a secret. at least at the start. For that we thank them. Those were the best of times for us - interacting with your officials, military and scientists. We are more interested in minds than bodies. Our interests as a race drifted away from the physical aeons ago. Now though, with more open contact with your people, we're forced to confront our own physicality again and rekindle a form of life we thought dead. We are being challenged by this touchy-feely world in other words.

It has led to clubs, where our race and yours interact (Wanting and not wanting to be a part of something - denial and affirmation interplay). It has also led to more emotional games that both our races deplore - gang warfare, with their humiliating initiation ceremonies - in other words, pride and shame - the temptation of forbidden fruit/ the betrayal of former allegiances: Wanting to be accepted by a new culture, so rejecting the old one and its values.

'Do-be-do, I want to be like you: Walk like you, talk like you'

We've found the simplest things explain best what

is happening between us and helps us understand you. Childhood games for instance, tells us about your adult games too - Catchings, Pass the Parcel (of responsibility), Snakes and Ladders, Cops and Robbers.

This mutual exchange has led to some ugly episodes - vivisection, botched plastic surgery to look like each other: We tell our young to use their minds, to alter how humans see them but they say that doesn't stop them seeing who they really are, when they look in the mirror. Thankfully we have machines that can mimic the anatomical appearance of other races and for some that is enough. For others though, even this doesn't satisfy them. For these beings, only transmigration of the soul fits the bill. Their spirits enter a human body and they know what it feels like to be truly human in every detail, even passing for Earth men in every facet of their lives.

Who can blame them for wanting to change?
"You smell!"
"God, you ugly little dwarves!"
"Your skin feels oily and horrible!"
"Why don't you talk like ordinary people do?" (We are telepaths with telekinetic abilities).
"How can you eat that disgusting mess?"
"Freaks!"
"Weirdos!"

Our culture, our beliefs are just too different for some people but thankfully not all. We found as a race that as we go through the universe, the universe goes through us and that things don't so much change as exchange. In other words, life is composed of two streams of reality - one coming, one going; one creating a new life for themselves and the other destroying their old one as they leave this existence.

This difference led to the alien riots, within a few years of our arrival as fear grabbed the local population and they saw only the negative aspects of about our being here.
"Our jobs, our health - who knows what diseases they carry?" They said about us, without a thought what illnesses they could pass onto us too (One sided, fear filled panic, ran riot). We became scapegoats for all their troubles and worries.

Time has moved on thankfully.

Now we can enjoy life here more as both the curiosity and prejudice have subsided somewhat. We now send out our own scientific expeditions across the World as well as into the oceans. We teach our ways to others and learn from them. We also send out missions to help heal the sick and improve the life of the poor, so ordinary people know we are here for them too and that there are advantages to letting us stay here, on this planet. It has been a bumpy ride but at last the storm over our presence is abating. I cannot promise your people or our own that new problems won't arise, only that we will do our best to overcome them and that it is to our mutual advantage to do so. The more our differences are explored and exploited, the better it will be for all concerned. That this cannot be rushed is also true (Everything has its time and pace to unfold).

We have had to accept that meeting in the middle, means lowering ourselves to humanities level and raising them to ours. It is a mutual educational program, where we descend into their hell and they rise to our heaven as it were (They become more sophisticated and we become more crude, in relationship to each other).

This is the sacrifice parents make for their children, women for their husbands and a failing civilisation makes for a rising one like yours. It is the way of the universe and all things bow to this reality because it has no choice in the matter. So we too accept our fate as you rebel against yours, to create your present life. We are your future as you are our past. The present is our common ground. This is the tragedy and the comedy of the situation - the horror and the humour, the knowing and not knowing, the wanting and not wanting. We have seen the light and now seek the dark, to rest in. We found eternity and journeyed through infinity - now seeking a finite life again.

Some day we'll integrate as the cultural and physical differences between us disintegrate. Now however the scars of this collision are too great, like the wounds an asteroid makes, when it collides with a planet's surface.

One day nobody will think that we are anything but 'human' and that's the irony of the current situation of distrust and hatred. As the two halves struggle now, they will in the future fight together as one, to protect their mutual home against a new foreign invader from out there and forget their past roles as enemies (estranged beings): 'A friend is an enemy that you haven't said good-bye to yet as an enemy is a friend you haven't said hello to' as our people say.

PRISONER OF PARADISE

Inside the green dome, No. 2 and his sidekick 31, are talking tactics for dealing with No. 6.

'We need to get him into the societal gaming network - make him believe things work one way, then tell him they work another way. Break him like a green branch, by pushing him one way then the other. Social metronomy in other words.'

'Good cop, bad cop you mean? Torture him until you get the truth out of him.'

'Don't be so naive 31. If you want the truth out of anybody, you get them to relax, think that they are safe. That's why the best spies are women.

No, torture is aimed at breaking a man's spirit, so that he'll grab any lifeline, any certainty - then you can mould him into anything you want. A man in pain will confess to anything - tell you whatever you want to hear, just to make it stop. You'll never get to the truth that way, in a month of Sundays. You can never be sure of any supposed secrets revealed that way. A broken man will be so grateful though, that he'll do anything for you.'

'The Stockholm Syndrome you mean?'

'Yes, they have such gratitude to the torturer because he's stopped that they end up loving him and become a convert to whatever cause he espouses. They would die for him. Slavish and brutish I know but it does the trick. A simple method. Get him to believe he fits in, break him of that belief, then reorientate again the way you want - hence 'The Three Layer Method."

In another part of The Village, away from the prying spyware and uncertain loyalty of fellow inmates, No 6 grooms his own protege.

'There are two types of people in this world, 13 - liars and truth tellers. Your lifelong task is to learn to distinguish between the two.'

'You mean lying Blackfeet and the honest Blackfeet?'

'Precisely. The people around you can be more dangerous to you than the obvious jailers. Is somebody too friendly, too prying? What are their motives for enquiry?

Those who hold us here, will try to confuse you and discourage any hope of escape and maybe they're right -

perhaps the only true escape is in your mind. They want to break you and reshape you to their will. If you want to be somewhere else, doing something else - they'll use that chink of weakness to get inside your head and crack it open like a walnut. You have to resist them and your own urge to run away, staying present no matter what. It's the only way for you, to stay you. Accept whatever is thrown your way and cope with it as best you can. That's the secret.

A corrupt society like this, wants to turn you into a mindless slave, a willing worker but not an intelligent one. Only the freedom to explore can break you of this insularity as an isolated individual - learning requires physical and especially mental movement. The irony is that a slave state dumbs itself down, ensuring its own demise because it is never prepared for anything that requires individual responsibility, reacting when it is too late, after orders eventually filter down from on high. A free society encourages the best out of people, not puts fear in. It motivates people to investigate, innovate - bringing out their true creative character, their individuality. All the things a slave society is afraid of. They don't want to delve and don't want others who work for them, to delve either. They hire those who are as corrupt as they are. Those too lazy and too cowardly, to probe the depths, so their personal secrets are left quietly buried.'

'How does that relate to this place then?'

'Lies. They say that they want to extract the truth from each and every one of us but do they? Maybe instead they are trying to bury the truth in our minds because in reality they are our old masters? All we see for sure are our fellows tortured and dumped, plus distrust fostered to keep us apart but are they forthcoming about anything to do with them?'

'No.'
'No. They lie to you, to manipulate you. They cite authority and the public good, for their actions, whereas the only motive for those who tell you the truth is to set you free from error, mistake. They want you to think things are calm, controlled, predictable - that there is nothing they haven't thought of and that they are in total charge of everything - God even but it is just a boring prison for the brain dead. They want you to feel safe or at least give up hope. That way they know you won't give them any trouble, by trying to escape. Don't question, don't struggle, don't fight - just submit and pretend to be happy, like some grotesque cages clown!'

With that 6 fell silent - angry at what he'd said, what he'd done and lost in fearful thought at his own predicament, like a fly trapped in a web.

ADVERTISING WORLD

"Say Bob, are you still using that same old car cleaner? What you need is to change to new, super-vibrant Slooms. You'll be glad you did!"

"Say Tom, did I see you painting your fence with that tired old set of brushes?"

"You sure did!"

"Then it's time you used Bristol pads, the most amazing painting system you'll ever find on this planet. What are you waiting for - buy it now! Success guaranteed or your money back. Call now! Remember this offer is not available in the shops."

"That's simply Amazing Bob!"

"Yes that's right. You'll never want to buy another painting system , once you've tried Bristol pads! But wait, there's more! If you buy one set today at this remarkable price, you get a second set absolutely free. Yes that's right - two for the price of one! There's even a thirty day money back guarantee. So buy today!"

"Wow!"

Suddenly a rocket taxi lands. They look at each other.

"It's the new neighbour," Bob says, looking down at his feet, sheepishly.

"It's like that is it?"

"Off-worlder."

"Oh." They stand in silence.

'Yes, scruffy, smelly. Doesn't go to the gym. Doesn't drive-"

"Doesn't drive! Is this guy crazy?"

Bob continued "Reads books-"

"No TV?"

"No TV."

"Is this guy weird or what?"

"I think they call them intellectuals."

"Geeks to us jocks."

"Christ!!"

"-And he doesn't go to church either or believe in God."

"What kind of animal are we dealing with here?"

"I don't know."

They part.

The following day they meet again.

"So Bob, how are you getting on with your new neighbour now?"

"Oh same as usual."   He puts his hands in his pockets. "Do you know he hasn't bought anything new since he got here."

"You're kidding?"

"No, he insists he likes his old products and it's all hogwash, this selling of newer and newer ones."

"This guy isn't real!"
"Says he's studying how we do things for his thesis,

whatever that is."

"Lookout, here he comes!"

"Hi Peter."

"Hello Robert."

"Do you know you'd be handsome if you shaved off that beard?"

"Is that so?"

"Yeh. What you need is Rapid Shave, Rough Cut - it ploughs through the toughest whiskers!"

"Cut the bullshit. I've heard it all before. By the way I'll decide if something is the best thing since sliced bread, not you. Emotive words and superlatives are mine to express or not, based on my own experiences. All these lies to sell things is a tragic waste of your time and mine."

"No need to be rude!" blurted out Tom.

Tom motioned him to be quiet.

"This is hardly a nice way to treat people, just trying

to be friendly."

"Your planetary government asked me here because they want your world to take a new direction - in fact they want to join us in outer space but realise that means ditching this materialistic, dead end existence."

"What do you mean by that?" queried Tom.

Again Bob signalled him to shut up.

"But why change a way of life that has sustained our planet for centuries?"

"Because it has more than sustained you. It has kept you in the dark - isolated and stuck in a time warp. You change continually but stay exactly the same - that is your paradox. You don't venture anywhere new, not even in your own minds. All you do is refine the same old things, over and over again."

"Why should that worry us?"

"Because as we've found on other planets we've visited, it doesn't last forever. Eventually it all implodes, when materials run out and minds become bored. Polluted resources, from the same substances being used over and over again, weakens them. Ideas repeated ad infinitum, do the same to minds. You have no choice - it's advance or stagnate and die."

"Well I don't like it!" said Tom.

"It doesn't matter what you like or don't like. Go back to sleep if you want but this world as a whole must wake up - if not it's doomed."

"Bull!"

"One day you'll find out the truth but by then it'll be too late for you as an individual. And some fell by the wayside...' he muttered to himself.

"What was that?"

"Nothing."

The planet did wake up of course. It stopped being bland and ineffectual. The old lies were dropped. People stopped believing in The Emperor's New Clothes Syndrome and saw the simple, obvious truth instead. It hurt their eyes initially but within a short space of time they adjusted to the new dream...

"Okay guys, how are we going to sell E = MC 2 to the public?"

ADDICTION

I am a monitor, class one. I have been on this planet for millennia. Sometimes I occupy the same body for a lifetime - at others for a short while, when collecting specific information. You are an interesting but doomed race. Soon you will have reached the point, where your renewable assets are as irreplaceable as your un-renewable ones and yet you carry on regardless.

We have seen this with other planets. They devour everything their world has to offer, then blame the victim for dying on them. It is a feeding frenzy that wipes out all life, including their own and turns their world into a hollowed out honeycomb, full of tunnels as they mine the mineral resources dry too. They cannot be stopped. They cannot be reasoned with because they assume that they are successful and have survived so far as they are right, not suicidal. An empty desert of a world is all they usually leave behind, like a plague of locusts. The few survivors left behind, do their best to scrape by in an almost untenable situation. We are such a race.

We've travelled the stars for aeons, assessing the survival rates of other races. We've watched as planet after planet has destroyed itself and come to the conclusion that we could have done nothing to stop our own people, let alone other world's populations. This addiction blinds us to the truth and turns us into unstoppable robots. Even after we've pushed ourselves to extinction, we still blame everyone and everything else for our demise: Those that were awake through all this or finally awoke to the folly of it, did the only thing they could - wept at the cost to their civilization and tried to adjust to the results (Picked themselves up, dusted themselves down and started all over again, where possible). Those you consider primitive people in your world are just such survivors, living a modest life until sober reality hits the rest of you.

We offer what help we can but we understand it must be to the right person at the right time. Some call us demons (the addicted) and some call us angels but we are just you from the future (tomorrow's ghosts). Like an electric shock, we enter your bodies and after we've left, you're left wondering what happened what happened when you were out. Some times you understand what we've done through you - other times not. You wake up to find the end results of our interference, in the form of words you cannot remember having written or actions that would make no sense to you, in what you consider conscious reality. We try to nudge you in the right direction - wake you up to possibilities but we cannot go against your free will as it is counter-productive (Life is voluntary after all as death (leaving) is obligatory: Nobody gets out of here alive). You must think and act for yourself or you will only blame us for the results, not moving on in conscious awareness but resisting our well meaning actions as a child does its parents (The rebel that wants to walk on its own two feet as a responsible adult and who are we to stop that?).

Even we do not understand everything. All we know is what we've found out about the bigger picture but things still elude our imagination. We see reality as a great, big system of creation and destruction that works on rules which can sometimes be changed and sometimes not. We cannot judge which is which, except in terms of failure or success. The Great Mystery is what draws us on - the puzzle that says 'don't interfere, just let things take their course and try to understand them. If we can save people it is because we are meant to and they want to join us on the great journey. If they spurn our assistance that is their choice and only the ego makes us want to force them to conform/ obey.

I have talked to you enough (you call it channelling). It is my turn to go elsewhere now and do other things. I have been given the call and must go. Au revoir (for now).

HOUSE MOUSE

'Get out and stay out!'

Robert looked out of his window. His neighbour was in his drive, surrounded by suitcases and other personal paraphernalia. He leaned out of the window.

'Thrown you out again?' He said, not so much as a question but as a statement of relentless fact. Bill was always getting thrown out of his own house and this was just another instance.

'I'd ask you in Bill but you know how it is?'

'Yeh, I know.' (Silence followed). 'How's Kate?'

'At her mother's. How's Sally?'

'At her mother's with the kids. I'll come out.'

They talked on Robert's drive.

'Damn these robot houses - who do they think they are?'

'Yeh but what can you do about it?'

'Not much.' Silence fell again.

'I'd heard that there was a revolt in Forbes Town.'

'Feeble. Waste of time.'

'What can we do about the situation?'

'Nothing it seems. They've taken over everywhere. They were meant to be our servants, not our masters.'

'Isn't that the problem though? We thought we could opt our of responsibility, by getting them to run everything for us sand now they have, including us.'

'Ain't that the truth!'

'We'll take care of you, they said and did. Free will is dangerous in the hands of children, who don't understand it.   We'll protect you - save you from yourselves.'

'Citizen, is everything okay?' A robotic black and white car had pulled up beside them, silently.

'You know the congregation of two or more human beings is prohibited by law?' It continued.

'Yes officer but my friend has just been thrown out of his house as you can see.'

A lazar beam scanned the suitcases.

'Even sot hat is no excuse.'

'I was offering to let him stay at my house, temporarily.' Robert said, trying not to let any emotion show because as he knew once registered as hostility, that would be it. Arrested as a subversive, taken into custody, questioned and 'altered' to make him a model citizen again. They'd seen it with Frank - taken away screaming and shouting one night,by the robotic police. Now he was back with a permanent smile on his face and no temper tantrums. No house would throw him out, ever. He was the perfect law abiding citizen since they'd messed around with his amygdala, the emotional centre of his brain.

'God,why do they keep us alive? Why do they need us?' he thought to himself and went back into his house with Bill.

'Billeting is allowed by law but only temporarily,

remember citizens.' The hollow, metallic voice reminded them, with all the concern of, well, a robot. All must be controlled, was the hive mind prime directive and all would be, eternally.

HOLE IN THE GROUND

'Stop!'
The shout rooted Martello to the spot.
'If you step forward, you'll regret it.'
'But it's only a puddle surely?'
'You're new here aren't you?'
'You mean this planet?'
'Yes, this planet.'
'Yeh but-'
'That puddle isn't a puddle.'
'What do you mean?'
'It's a portal to another dimension.'
'How do you know?'
'My people have observed this phenomena for many years. We have seen rocks, animals, people fall in and never come out again. We have also had to put up with what came through from the other side.'
'Like what?'
'Things' He gave a shudder.
After a few seconds he went on again.
'Once a horrible, black slug like creature got into our world. We eventually killed it but not before it had killed and eaten many of our people. We didn't realise it was there for a start because it hid from the harsh light and heat of the day. There have been other, similar monsters too. Then there was the invasion. People like us but organised into a relentless and ruthless army. We

capped that hole after fighting them off but who knows if they'll come back and where? Maybe next time we won't be so lucky and they'll chose a remote location or come through several portals at once.'

'Does nobody who has fallen through return?'

'Sometimes bits of of people or animals reappear but they are not a pretty sight. We always assume one of those slug like creatures or worse got them.'

'Why don't you fill in the holes?'

'Because they are bottomless. we cap them but even then it can be counter-productive as cutting off the light seems to make them grow because they swallow whatever is put on top of them.'

'What about digging underneath them?'

The alien looked at Martello in a world-weary kind of way, like an old man talking to a child.

'My people did dig below one. What they found was that it was like looking through a hole in the ground, up into the sky but deadly.'

'Deadly?'

'Yes. One guy tried to put his hand through and his whole arm disappeared.'

'Nasty!'

'He was none to pleased!' The old man gave a grim chuckle.

'Snyppe, what have you been telling our off-world guest?' A smart suited person, interrupted the conservation.

'About the holes.'

The new alien turned to Martello.

'You didn't believe a word that old joker said, did you? He plays tricks on all visitors like you. Nasty psychological fun, according to him'

The old man shrugged his shoulders.

'You can step into the puddle with no worries - it is just water after all.'

Martello did just that, laughing at having been taken in and instantly vanished without a trace.

'I told you before old man - this is our business. Don't betray our secrets to off-worlders or next time I might put you down that goddam hole too!' The secret policeman walked off and Snyppe finished his drink, before heading home from the cantina.

'Politeness.' Was all he said before disappearing down the dusty road.

DA-LEK!

"The in-dig-ni-ty! The in-dig-ni-ty!!"
The dalek railed against the state it found itself in. Like some circus freak in aside show, it found itself trapped in a horrific dimension of powerlessness.

In a few minutes some human idiot would pay the credits necessary and out he'd roll again, firing blanks and shouting all kinds of obscenities at those that had captured this virulent tin bucket.

"Death to all hu-mans!"
"A-ttack! A-ttack!"
"Ex-ter-mi-nate! Ex-ter-mi-nate!"

How did he manage to get immobilised and captured, he wondered? There was a big explosion, his gun ceased functioning and a giant rock crushed him against the ship. The battle moved on but he stayed jammed where he was, rusting in anything but peace. Years passed. Dirt and dust built up on his carapace. He watched and waited, until the mess eventually covered his eye stick. At this point he shut down and went into hibernation mode. He'd hoped that he could have self destructed but the radiation blast had disabled this function and many others.

According to the dalek survival manual, no member of his race was ever finished - no matter what state it found itself in or where. It could shut down, reawaken and replicate itself as a fifth columnist behind enemy lines.

When the scrap metal merchant arrived, millenia later, they had no idea who or what he was. This was a lifeless moon and he was just another piece of waste metal (like his ship) that they could sell on: The universe is so vast and old that newer races and civilisations are always discovering remnants of bygone eras and errors - so much so that they had become blase about it.

And now here he was - sold to a games arcade manager, on a dump of a planetoid, who recognised this tin pot monster for what it was.
"Yeh, I'll give you ten credits for this rust bucket."
"It's worth more than that!"
"Who to, a museum? No, ten credits or you can dump it where you usually dump such rubbish, Jago."
"Fifteen or I'll never come here again!"
"Is that a promise?"
"Branket!"
"Temper, temper! Eleven as I know you, no more because I know you too well."
They shook (Their bodies with rage, not their hands

in agreement). Money was exchanged and they parted.

"A dalek - what a prize! You'll look good in the central arcade, beside that other rusting hulk of a Zircon war robot. Now a little bit of spit and polish, and you'll be fine!"

So it came to pass...
"I hate hu-mans! I hate hu-mans! Free me from these re-straints and I'll show you what a da-lek is made of!"
"I don't think so. That's almost human sentiment, my friend."
"Friend? Friend? I am not your friend! I am a da-lek, you're mor-tal en-e-my!"
"Settle down, you're not going anywhere. Your gun is plugged and we're going to have a long and fruitful association."
"The in-dig-ni-ty! The in-dig-ni-ty!"

After a thousand years, another dalek battle cruiser appeared on the horizon, destroying the arcade and most of the rest of the transport cafe complex that made up what little life existed on the planetoid. It accidentally freed the dalek too, which spent the rest of its existence, roaming the now lifeless world.
"The in-dig-ni-ty! The in-dig-ni-ty!" It ranted, lost in the eternal insanity of its hurt pride.

THE THREE ALIENS

Hear No Evil, See No Evil and Speak No Evil, visited Earth.

They looked upon the works of humanity and said:-
'I can't see what all the fuss is about.'
'I don't hear anything worth listening to.'
Speak No Evil said nothing.

They came to a wasteland of polluted filth, killed off by industrial chemicals.
'I can't see anything wrong with all this disrespect of the environment.'
'I can't hear any bird songs, which always irritated me about this planet anyway.'
Speak No Evil said nothing.

Taking off in their spaceship, they surveyed the landscape below, where a battle was taking place and people were dying in their thousands.
'It looks like it is all their own fault.'
'I hear no voices of dissent.'
Speak No Evil said nothing.

On they moved to another land, where water was scarce, crops had failed and people were starving to death in their hundreds of thousands.

'I see overpopulation and failure to plan,' said See No Evil.

'I've heard nothing to contradict this.'

Speak No Evil said nothing.

They came to a new land - again where suffering was rife. A plague had descended upon the people and many were dying in agony.

'I see nothing to concern us here.'

'Others tell me it is their failure at general hygiene level - they've brought this on themselves.'

Speak No Evil said nothing.

They decided to get closer to the land but before they could take their ship down, an immense storm devastated the topics below them, drowning many people and destroying the infrastructure.

'I see the same problem occurring over and over again - why don't they plan better for them?'

'I hear they are not much into forward planning and consider it The Supreme Beings fault that this happens.'

Speak No Evil said nothing.

The instruments on their ship displayed major seismic disturbances, to the west of their location.

Buildings fell, people were crushed and general mayhem followed.

'I don't see any lessons learnt from the past here, about natural disasters.'

'I've heard nothing from other visitors to this planet, that show building construction techniques have improved over the centuries.'

Speak No Evil said nothing.

Later they took their craft down again, to ground level and viewed life in more detail, using techniques of invisibility to move freely amongst the crowds. Violent crime, civil unrest, sick people dying on the streets, drug and alcohol abuse, sexual disease running rampant...

See No Evil shook his head and looked at Hear No Evil, who threw up his hands in despair. Both looked at See No Evil, who said nothing.

www.ingramcontent.com/pod-product-compliance
Lightning Source LLC
Chambersburg PA
CBHW071012120726
47910CB00004B/1488